THE LETTER

* Fragments of my Soul *

Samuel Onyeche

Ukiyoto Publishing

All global publishing rights are held by

Ukiyoto Publishing

Published in 2023

Content Copyright © Samuel Onyeche

ISBN 9789359204291

All rights reserved.
No part of this publication may be reproduced, transmitted, or stored in a retrieval system, in any form by any means, electronic, mechanical, photocopying, recording or otherwise, without the prior permission of the publisher.

The moral rights of the author have been asserted.

This book is sold subject to the condition that it shall not by way of trade or otherwise, be lent, resold, hired out or otherwise circulated, without the publisher's prior consent, in any form of binding or cover other than that in which it is published.

www.ukiyoto.com

The Letter

Fragments of my Soul

SAMUEL ONYECHE

to all young people all over the World

Acknowledgements

The wisdom that births knowledge, the muse that births creativity, and the thought that births tangible things are but gifts from the Almighty God. I return all the Glory to him; whose healing leaves no scar. With the face of a thousand joy, I say thank you to my lovely parents; Mr. and Mrs. Jonathan Onyeche, and to my ever-caring sister; Joy Chidinma Tochuwkwu. May the Good Lord greatly reward all of you for your incessant support, love, and encouragement.

As the wings of the great eagle are made up of different strands of individual feathers, so is my writing journey, and as such; I am very grateful to my mentors and academic fathers: Prof. Kontein Trinya, Prof. Samuel Otamiri, Prof. Samuel Amaele, Prof. Ibiere Ken-maduako (My Academic mother) , Prof. Jawaz Jaffri (Pakistan). Dr. Anthony Orlu, Dr. Wellington Nwogu, Dr. Uzo Nwamara and Dr. Ibiwari Ikiriko.

I passionately, press the trigger of a thousand gunshots (of gratitude), as I say thank you to poet Francis Otole, poet John Chinaka Onyeche, Poet Saro Ogumba, Uncle Philip Amadi Mr. Promise C J, Engr. Abinye D. C. Nwankwo, Aunty Boma Samuel, Nket Godwin, Mr. Jacob Irikana, Miss Ella C. Uchendu, and my lovely friend; Miss Goodness Obinnah. My success story can not be told without their names being mentioned. I am so blessed to have these amazing people in my life.

Finally, I am very grateful to Sedar Samuel; my unborn child, who miraculously happens to be the muse of this life-transforming book. Dear Sedar wherever you are in the world of the unborn, I want you to know that Daddy loves you and can't wait to behold your face and bear you in his lovely arms.

From The Writer...

As graveside songs require no dancer
So also is this letter I write to you
For the melody of dirges are no melody
But drops of sorrow woven into stanzas.
As the gravewall is not built of brick
But concrete grief sheltering the dead
So are the poems I poem of you
These songs you sing are no song
Neither is tears a conglomeration
Of flowers embroidered to flatter—
Each drop of ink, each weld of words
Each sound, each echo, each morph
Each rhyme, each rhythm, each figure
Are but the fragments of my soul
Melted into letters inked with blood.

Samuel Alozie Onyeche
Port Harcourt, Nigeria 2023

Contents

Words For The Wise	1
Preface	2
Praise for the Book	4
The Letter	7
Son	14
Freedom	16
The Act of Seduction	18
If You Fall Forty Times	23
Things a Man Should Fear	25
When Marriage Calls	28
How to find a Perfect Woman	30
The Tongue of a Woman	32
Two Heavens	36
The Fate of the Wicked	37
Final Words...	39
Glossary	43
About the Author	44
Books by the Author	47

Words For The Wise

The worst prisons are not built with bricks neither
is the strongest form of slavery made of chains.

Preface

The art of writing has been a natural phenomenon among writers, from the time of William Shakespeare, Aristotle, and Plato, to the time of Abraham Lincoln, Napoleon Hill, George Orwell, Léopold Sédar Senghor, Okot p'Bitek, Flora Nwapa, Chinua Achebe, Wole Soyinka, Chimamndah Ngozi Adichie and to many contemporary writers.

Literature has been used as a weapon to fight societal decadence, it also serves as a tool with which cultural values, ethics, good morals, virtues are instilled in the lives of people, most importantly the younger generation. Literature (Poetry) is a powerful tool for emancipation. This assertion was proven in the mid-1950s when poets like Langston Hughes, Claude McKay, Helene Johnson, Anne Spencer, and some others used their poems to fight in the Civil Rights.

In the same vein this book is a timely response to the societal cancers eating up the body of our world. It is no longer news that the rate of teenage pregnancy, prostitution, abortion, addiction, theft, drug abuse, examination malpractice, arm robbery, internet fraud, and all forms of corrupt practices have become the order of the day, these are traumatic issues, we can not afford to ignore.

" The Letter" was born out of burden, and concern for the youths and teenagers all over the world, most especially those who do not have people to advise, direct and mentor them, who are daily struggling to navigate through the storms of life on their own, in a world full of societal decadence, street to street violence, cultism, peer pressure, poverty, inflation, joblessness and unhealthy competitions which have become the invisible vipers sucking decency out of our world.

On the other hand, Most parents are always busy trying to provide for the family, Many leave the house as early as 5am and return 9pm thereby having little or no time to raise their children. A quote by Prof. Kontein Trinya says" Do not grow up be raised". The holy Bible in Proverbs 22:6 Also emphasizes the significance of training a child, it says : "Train up a child in the way he should go, And when he is old he will not depart from it". Well raised children bring joy and peace to their parents but children left on their own is like the proverbial rabbit that brings fire and smoke into a communal burrow.

This book is but life's compass, an embodiment of divine wisdom, filled with life transforming teachings and aphorisms. it is a route to knowledge, wealth, longevity and peace of mind to anyone who reads, and obeys the precepts therein.

Praise for the Book

Fragments of the poet's soul, deep and heavenly-inspired drops of wisdom cinched by words artistically hammered and smelted into stanzas by a crafty wordsmith.

— Prof Ibiere Ken-Maduako

Department of English and Communication Art, Ignatius Ajuru University of Education, Port Harcourt, Nigeria.

THE LETTER is a book with many brooks; a summon with sermons, a teaching with preaching. It is a mine of wisdom, and an ocean with depth of insights. It is a manual for sound health and genuine wealth. It offers guide to life and success. It exposes the easiest way to man's ruin and the path that leads to shame and flame. THE LETTER is a tour-de-force that has consolidated Samuel Onyeche as a Master of Word Art, a skillful craftsman who knows how to chisel with pen, a poet to be admired among men in the services of the Muse. A poet; colourful, brilliant, witty and compelling.

— Francis Otole

Earth. Poet & Author of Heaven is a Place on Earth.

"In the epistolary poetry, entitled, The Letter, Samuel Onyeche inventively provides some parabolic pieces of advice to his unborn son; a synecdoche that he employs to reflect and affect the lives of both teenagers and youths of the contemporary time and those afterwards…the intellectual stride of the writer, no doubt, is profoundly phenomenal."

— *Wellington Nwogu, PhD*
Author of Dark Rhythms and Director, Purple Letters Publishers, Port Harcourt.

"Here's a collection of poetic nuggets from a prolific poet, who uses the voice of the poet persona to advise his imaginary son on some existential issues via an epistolary form. The poems in this collection are both didactic and dramatic, and as such could be read for their enlightening or entertaining values. In any case, they should be read by young people, who aspire to attain great heights in life and their parents also."

Humphrey Ogu
Poet, short fiction writer, playwright and journalist; Vice Chairman, Association of Nigerian Authors (ANA) Rivers State.

Samuel Onyeche, the author, is a gifted and intellectual writer. He addresses a number of serious issues in this letter to his unborn son. The biggest handicap in life is having a mentality that does not think critically. He made the observation that virtue does not grow on trees. That sensible son should be aware that while courage is a pillar, fear is a destroyer. Those who put courage before fear are heroes. Pride, desire, gluttony, and friends who are really just wolves in sheep's clothing are some things you should, however, fear. These and many other things are revealed in this letter.

Samuel remarked that the distinction between freedom and madness was tenuous. Therefore, you shouldn't be seduced by the freedom a crazy man has to dance naked on the street. Do not envy others; their freedom may be your undoing. The book also discusses relationships; marriage is not for the learned man who can list the botanical names of every insult and plot the graphs of retaliation analytically. Think you will find a lot more nuggets in this open letter.

Engr. Abinye D.C. Nwankwo
Author of: Train Me.

In _*THE LETTER, *_ Samuel Onyeche didn't just pen down beautiful words. In these beautiful words, lies priceless gems that will make young Sedar so rich, in character and conduct. If you're young, uncover this Treasure Chest, get rich with Sedar.

Woruka, Deborah O.
Blogger / Poet / Educator

The Letter

An Epistolary poetry,
Port Harcourt; Nigeria.
March 2023.

My Dear Son,
How are you coping with the daily battles and struggles that life frequently throws at you?
Great winner of many battles past— Victor of
many more to come. Sedar my beloved son
I write to you, for it is not only the neck of a
cadaver that needs to be straightened no! no!
The neck of the living needs such favour the most.
For the butterfly that has no adviser dies in a
spider's spinneret and the farmfly that heeds
not to warning; weeps in regret and dies in the
ground, alongside its bait: the farmer's defecate.
Hence, I write you this letter; a compass of life.
My son, listen to the voice of wisdom and make
its precepts your life's manual. For virtues do not

grow on trees, courage is not a chocolate candy
purchased from the superstore, neither is knowledge
a seastone, carelessly picked by frolicking fingers.
Kiss the lips of knowledge, fall in love with wisdom
for wisdom is the fire that refines men, true wisdom
is a gift, only God can give. Only God can give.
Wise orphans zestfully plant their ears inside good
advice— learning from the lips of others' parents
Feeding their brain with the bread of wisdom. For life
becomes cruel when eyes lack clue. Life becomes hell
when ears refuse to hear, when ears refuse to hear.

> The greatest disability
> Is not the prickled eyes that see not
> Nor the deafened ears that hear not
> It is not the lame legs that walk not
> Nor the paralysed hands that hold not
> The greatest disability in life
> Is that of the mind, that thinks not wisely
> For men certainly become their thought—
> But woe awaits those whose hearts
> are the farmland of crooked thoughts.

Life is a farmland; thoughts are seeds, what you

Sow you shall reap. Be careful of what grows in you
Be very mindful of the species of your thoughts, for
thoughts are the metaphors of what we become
A failed life is the offspring of a failed mindset:

> "If you think you're beaten, you are.
> If you think you dare not, you don't.
> If you like to win, but think you can't,
> It's almost a cinch you won't
> Life's battle doesn't always go
> To the stronger or Cast man;
> But soon or late the man who wins
> Is the one who thinks he can".
> ------**Walter D. Wintle.**

My son, listen to the wealthy words of this didactic letter
feed your mind with its teachings and eat the sweetness
of its bitter truths. For the bitterness of truths are herbs
that cure blindness and set ignorance ablaze—
Men become blind and eternal slaves when their
dirty desires remote their actions, be mindful of this—
Be the master of your mind, the chef of your thoughts.

The Letter

Plant not your young eyes in another man's pocket

nor fantasize about the nudity of another man's bride

for these are the doors that lead to an early grave;

the blades that reduce kings and queens to toothpicks.

Never you admire the vain pleasures of these paths

for the dungeon therein is a baseless pit, pit of agony

that makes great men live dead lives, and turn kings into slaves.

Do not dine with the shallow-minded or with those who

Had buried their heart in the belly of rocks— men who

do not sleep unless they take what belongs to the poor.

Dream not dreams with men whose hearts lack clemency

lest they afflict you with their deadly diseases. Be wise

be humble, be gentle but ambitious, be gentle but rugged

be polite but brave; never plant all your hope as seeds

on the palm of trusted friends, for not all madmen are

insane, not all sane men are truly sane. Be an ant; be a

scholar, make love to wisdom; let nature be your teacher.

Beware of friendly foes
For If an enemy seeks your head
An enemy, your head, you may escape

If a vampire comes for your blood
A vampire your blood
You may overcome

But when your friend plots your death,
Your Brutus your death plots
Only heaven can tell your fate.

Love your friends as you love your foes, do not name a tree by the colour of its leaf, for life is like a chameleon; its skin has no label, so wolves wear doves to the feast of doves. My son, never swallow another man's spittle or fear the cold flames in a foe's eyes, for fear is a killer and courage, a pillar. But "cowards die many times before their death" while the courageous see several scenting seasons, overcome countless deaths, and win many wars.

Give compassion the rooms in your heart, be kind but Wise; be a dove, be an Ajuala (the gentle serpent that strikes after seven counts, whose venom has no cure). Be wise lest your kindness bring you swarm of scorpions.

Do not drink from people's tears, nor fish in the river of anyone's sorrow, for such fishes bring wealth that carries curses in their belly. Curses that kill the blessed; wealth that withers like grass, planting plenty plants in the fertile farm of karma, plants that bear cursed fruits for your offspring to plunk and wail. Such fruits befit you not.

It is best for witches and wizards, quenchers of lights, masters of medicine – medicine that mars lives.

Such cursed fruits befit you not, my son. It befits you not.

Wash your palm in the bowel of your conscience, let the

voice of your conscience keep you clean. Never you spit

on the simple or knock down the noble or ride on the horse

whose back is broken, for these acts lead to the throne of thorns. Feed your sight with the herbs in these words,

and also feed your soul with the meal of the Holy Word of God,

for life becomes cruel when eyes lack clue; life becomes

hell when ears refuse to hear; when ears refuse to hear.

Son

Be mindful of the beauty of flowers especially
(Roses and Jasmines)- these are pretty plants
That bear no fruit, herbs that heal only the dead

But blossom than the blooms of a male pawpaw tree

Be careful of words shot from the gun of desire

They are fiercer than the missiles of Amadioha, fear

These bullets: (covenant & oats) and others like it.

They kill a child when his life begins to taste delicious

Make no vow in times of anger, no promise in passion pressure

For unspoken words can be retrieved, but who can retrieve

What the sun has swallowed? Who can travel into the

intestines of time, to bring back the vapor of verbal verbs.

Be mindful of the beauty of a maiden's breast, beware of

The dirty desire that comes at the sight of pretty nipples.

No wise man embraces beauty in a hurry- for beauty is a

weapon and wisdom; a gift that frightens... even gods.
Do not build seats on the anthill of love or weave
garlands with the beauty of reeds, for the reed of
L-o -v - e is thorn and the anthill, scorpion's sting.
Do not plant emotion on the
      a i r
Neither cultivate feelings in the fine farm of lust
For feelings will grow old and die, emotions will

              E
          S
      I   and   F
   R   A
                           L
                                L

But their scars forever remain.

Freedom

The worst prisons are not built with bricks neither is
The strongest form of slavery made of chains. There
is a thin line between freedom and insanity, beware!
My son. Only the insane are free, free to dance naked
In the marketplace, only the madwoman is free, free
to flaunt the beauty of her breast in an open field,
Only the madmen are free to naked the three gods
In between their legs and dangle them shamelessly
in the village square of a thousand eyes and pay no fine
None takes him to court for committing sacrilege
My son let not the insane freedom you see in the streets
entice you. Do not open your eye's door to the insanity
of bare breasts, wielding two pointed missiles of mass
destruction. These seductions you see are a fisher's line
It ends with a beautiful bait that wears doom.

Do not open your heart's door to the insanity of tempting

shapes; beautiful Delilahs sampling nuclear nipples of

destiny destruction. This beauty you see is a fisher's line,

It ends with a magnificent bait that wears death.

The Act of Seduction

A beautiful lady; a lonely room, a beautiful body smiling at you, red tempting lips; hot hips; short gown, half

clothed boobs; pointed nipples, staring you in the face.

Oily lips, tongue rolling with desire-intoxicated eyes

Moaning mouth of cravings --- opening and closing—

Sweet silent whispers calling your name, shifting towards you

hungry for your tender touch, thirsty for a kiss, Inviting you

with a soft violin voice, she whirls and whispers "do not be

 afraid, I have locked the door, no one is here— just you and I.

Come handsome one, come let us go to heaven. Don't you want to be there? Haven't you heard of its beauty and

bliss? Let us go to this heavenly place, where honey flows

like streams— and pleasure burns wild, like harmattan fire

Come let's swim in the stream of sweetness and fly as we

Scream, moan, and groan on the bed of perfect pleasure".

Flee my son, flee like Joseph to save your bright future

For her pleasure is the dungeon of death, and her heaven, hell

Flee my son, this is the act of seduction; the call of death, my son

    When death calls at night
    With the voice of a violin
    On the waist of a pretty fruit tree

    Do not answer, do not
    Twice look, for that is relish
    And relish is pleasure
    And the pleasure of lust is death

    My son, do not desire
    The beautiful boobs of a tree
    Whose root taps life from death.

The Letter

Seeing is different from looking, the mad woman's nudity

Intoxicates no sane man. Is she not a woman? My son

Seeing is different from looking, the eye is no sin, but a

second look is. Tame your mind; the engineer of thoughts

the womb of all actions, for sin stands now at the nose

of every street, dragging great men to their early graves.

Be mindful of the maiden that invites you for a dinner

Staring at you with a trailer load of desire— eyes of lust

Be careful of the bare beauty her curvy body portrays

For some beauty carry cruel curses in their kisses and

in a few lie life, fortune, and peace. Be wise for tears,

shame and death is the name of the housefly, that hovers

over the household of men whose third legs lack control.

>Sedar my son, be not in a hurry
>There is a time for everything
>A season for everyone
>Beauty for every face
>Smile for every cheek

Joy for every heart

There is a time for everything
A groom for every bride
A bride for every groom
Food for every stomach
Sky for every bird
Please wait for the right time.

My Son, I have seen several sides to life, several sides to life have I seen. I have seen the back of the clock; the spirits of insanity know my name I have lived behind the market, within the market and inside the market, trust me life is beautiful, life is war— she stood as twin lion on my path— A wrestling match came to me by force, a match not fit for men, I fought at infant, I fought with forbidden freedom, I fought, I wailed, I saw a skull of fire, I saw the world in walls, I know the mysteries of beautiful rags, I know why parrots live in the lips of madmen, and why jealousy kills faster than a bullet, I know why bitter medicine leaves its footprints on the teeth of a sick child.

The Letter

For I have seen several sides to life, several sides
to life have I seen. Life is beautiful life is war. But
he who puts God first in all he does, obeying all his
ordinances shall never see shame. He shall not
die like the grasshopper caught by a spider's web
neither shall he die like the motherless chick—
Scratching the soil for food and suddenly, scooped
and devoured by the claws of hungry hawks.

If You Fall Forty Times

My son do not fear the sun or dread the moon, for
Heroes are Men and Heaven is a Place. Heroes are
Men who choose courage over fear and Heaven is
a Place; build one for yourself.
When you fall, rise! If you fall again, rise again!
If you fall forty times, rise forty one times. Rise!
If you make mistake, forgive yourself; learn and
move on. Move on. Do not draw maps of circles
to hide your errors, strike a stroke and move on.
I, too, fell, failed, cried and rose a thousand times,
If you fall forty times, rise forty one times. Rise!
I, too, once drew maps of circles against the faces
of my mistakes, but I learnt, I learnt that in covering
 a mistake maps and thick circles mar the page.
Sedar my son, mistakes are no crime, strike a stroke
and move on. But don't repeat the same mistake twice.
Don't, don't.
For when a repeated mistake grows Iroko roots

It evolves into trees of tares, tares you can't uproot
So "study to show yourself approved, the son of
Samuel that needs not to be ashamed". I call you
Sedar: He who shall not be humiliated, he who shall
not be mocked not even in a song, not even at your
back, not even when I'm gone, not even at your death
Study, my son. study, for the wilderness is not the
waterless world where nothing that flows flows; where
Nothing that grows grows; where nothing that sings sings

Wilderness is that empty skull wearing ignorance with pride.

Things a Man Should Fear

There are things a man should fear, fear them without phobia. Do not share a bed with them,
for madness begins with common laughter.

*Fear Pride**
Fear it without phobia for she is a serial killer;
a lethal sickness that doctors cannot diagnose

*Fear lust**
For no madness is greater. Many mighty men she reduces to toothpick, many virtuous women he turns to fools. Lust wears its victim rags and blinds them from seeing it, it crowns them with songs of shame and make them dance their doom Fear lust, she is a beautiful python; her belly is the graveyard of many great dreams; the graveyard of many beautiful lights not allowed to shine

*Fear food**
A glutton's death lies in his throat. Fear food, fear food; eat wisely. A swollen death is not fit for kings, a poisoned meal bears the fattest meat, a poisoned

meal bears the most palatable aroma, an aroma that
can make even the dead salivate– the trap set for fools

Fear friends*

For the true ones are rare, some are foes and
Friendship— a mask; the enemy's flower of beautiful wiles.

Fear money*

For the love of it is a sexy snare. Fear money, hunt it
more than me. Let its love kill the laziness in you
But never value money over health, never trade loved ones
Or humanity for wealth, for wealth gotten in blood
is like the elation of partying rats—eating and rejoicing
over a table of poisoned food— the consequences of
ignorance.

Fear love and dread beauty*

For a beautiful woman's eyes are ancient spells
strong as thánatos. In those eyes lies the grave
of Sampson, David and Solomon. Fear this and
many more like it, do not share a bed with them,
for the sharing of a bed leads to a touch, a touch
leads to romance, romance to kisses, and from
kisses, fornication is born — the grave of the anointed.

Fear untimely love and dread tempting beauty-
For madness begins with mere laughter and
in such beauty lies Mturufe; the hidden snare that
that kills the wise, the earthen wire worse than a
sniper's shot. Beware of this and many more like it,
For these are the doors that lead the ignorant to
their green graves; the home of premature death.

When Marriage Calls

My Son, never marry because of mates
A life lived in competition wins medals of agony
Never marry because of beauty,
For beauty is temporary, looks are lairs
Never marry because of lack or its opposite
For love built on this is like a mansion built
on a tree, it will collapse when the wind whirls
Never marry shambling feet— daughters of Jezebel.
A lazy woman's cooking pot is a boiling nail
Her meal is never ready, never served
She never quenches her husband's hunger
At the dawn of his yawning mouth
Her fine feet are hard labour to her moves
Her farm is the dance floor of wild weeds
Where odu and ebi play hide and seek.
Wash your eyes well in the river of wisdom
Search for a wife in the family of virtues
Not in the charming boutique of beauty
Beauty borrowed from Foundation, Bronzer,

Samuel Onyeche

Mascara and Eyelashes. The beauty of dust
that quickly fades like shore-sand sculpture.
My son, when marriage calls, pray and cry to
the Almighty God, for Him alone gives gifts,
beautiful gifts that bring no tears, no regrets.
Listen, my son, every woman is a builder; some
build your libido in a matter of months, turning
you into a pintle-pundit. Every woman is a builder;
some build your bank account into hallow holes
Emptying your dream and your life on the spot
Every woman is a builder; some build animosity
into your family ties — separating you from your
root, cutting you off from your source.
Every woman is a builder; some build failures
Transforming them into legends, raising drunks to sit
With kings. My son, my son, every woman is a builder.
Be careful when handling these delicate creatures,
for in them is the handsomeness of a man; in them
is the joy of a man; in them is the life of a man; in them
is the woe of a man; in them is the early grave of a
million men.

How to find a Perfect Woman

My son, as there is no beautiful flesh in the grave,
as there is no flawless man in the universe,
So also there is no perfect woman on earth.
He who desires a perfect woman is like a child
searching for the mother's breastmilk on his father's
chest. He who longs for a perfect woman is like
the wise fool digging oceans in search of honey
My son, there are perfect pulchritudes, yes there are.
There are perfect shapes, perfect dimples, perfect eyes
Perfect nostrils, perfect lips, perfect boobs, perfect hips.
But hear this truth, my son, there is no perfect woman
He who finds a woman whose love is genuine as truth
He who finds a woman whose ways are lucid as glass
He who finds a woman whose heart is fragile as flowers
He who finds a woman whose anger is transient as dew
He who finds a woman whose words are kind as herbs

He who finds a woman whose action is laced with love

He who finds a Godly woman whose love is impeccable

As the sun, love that falls not for wealth— imgullable love.

Who can find a woman with all these qualities? Who ?

For life is a crafty giver--- no single tree possesses all fruits.

He who craves for bewitching beauty shall find. He who

desires a virgin shall find. He who craves for wealth

may find, he who wants intelligent woman shall also find.

But none of this is greater than the peace of mind a

good woman gives. My son, search for peace of mind

for therein lies love, elation, rest, and blissful longevity.

The Tongue of a Woman

My son, my son, my son
How many times did I call?
Listen,
This house was a hut
It is your mother who made it home.
That kitchen was made of mud, she made it a place of strength,
I was nobody, just a lonely poet... Now look around
look at cars, look at you, look at mansions.
She gave me a family, peace, and love.
The beauties of a good woman is beyond words,
 beyond men, beyond gods--
But listen, my son
The tongue of a woman is like the sting of scorpions;
the missile of stinging bees; the true definition of pain.
still, they are the honey of life, the hub of happiness.
The pintle of a hornet yet, the solace of broken days.
My son when the demons in her head have risen,
when thunder and arrows shoot from her tongue,
when her anger uncoils like a provoked python

Do not be wise, do not be mighty, do not your strength show.

Lest you bury your God-given treasure

In a beautiful casket carved by anger.

For marriage is not for the wise, who number the pain of every hurt, calculating the altitude of each wrong. Marriage is not for the wise, who write the name of every offence; plotting heart-graphs of red revenge. Marriage is not for the wise, whose smile hold many imageries of grief; the grief of unforgiveness that sets snares of atomic animosity on the length of years Marriage is not for the wise, whose heart is the canvas of a calabash upon which horror is etched. horrors holding vengeance in their hands. Marriage is not for the wise whose heart is a bottle-like diary: the prisoner of many names, prisoner of many dark places; the art of witchcraft, ways of the stone-hearted Marriage is not for the wise, who know the value of every grain, always hunting to gather every gain, not willing to sacrifice, not ready to tolerate, not willing to forgive, not ready to apologize. Marriage is not for the wise. It is for those whom the world calls fools, whilst they are the wisest of the wise. The holy book says so.

But hear this, my son, love is a mystery; who can wholly fathom it? Who can claim to know it all? Who can boast

of its mastery? Love is a hard nut; the one you love dearly

May not love you, but loves another dearly, and the pretty

damsel who loves you dearly, may not be the one you love.

This thing called love is a mystery; who can totally fathom it?

Hear this truth, my son: If you are not loved by love,

even if you grow as a promising plant amongst weeds,

Among thistles and thorns, you will be called a wild

Weed; the fate of a weed will be your fate. If you

are not loved by love, even though you swim the sea's

depth and fetch her the ornaments of the ocean, the

pride of the sky and the glory of the moon, buy her

jewelries of gold and bracelets of diamond, the fate

of a millipede will still be your fate. If you are not loved by

love, even though you struggle into the cloud and pluck

her the shining moon, decorate her name with sporting

stars, the fate of a cockroach will be your fate, for love, care, and attention are valued when given to those who truly deserve them.

Two Heavens

Do not think of owning two gardens
that is but the wisdom of the weak,
the strength of a coward.
There are benefits of owing two gardens
One on the right and the other on the left.
How can a such person catch cold at night?
There are beauties of owing two he(a)vens.
My son, do not let men deceive you
heaven is beautiful, heaven is wonderful
heaven is admirable.
It has everything you could ever imagine
including hell, for he who entangles himself
With two heavens gets the bonus of a dozen
hell.

The Fate of the Wicked

My Son, life is a seed and harvest— a must
Be careful my son and harm no man, defraud
No man, poison no man, envy no man, kill
No man— envy not those who excel in evil
Evil is a tree that never bears good fruit
Even when her twigs hawk beautiful fruits
Jealous it not, for the wind will blow it brutally
Karma worms will invade, for karma is a
faithful visitor and evil; a tree that bears harm
Yesterday, I saw the witchdoctor's children
Streams of sympathy drenched my heart
I did not cry but tears flowed down my chin.
For their visage could make stones sob
The witchdoctor's children are like stunted
anthills --- GLORIFIED PIGS— who scavenge not
only the bins, but also rabbit holes and
people's homes, pregnant pots grow leopard
legs and never return.

The wizard and witch doctor's children are
beer beetles, bees without honey, they are
hungry hornets. Dare not dine with them—
for the silva of ghosts is like a viper's vemon.
Dare not fight with them a mere push, can
make you a murderer, for they are ghosts in
human skin, they died long time ago, they died
in their father's evil deeds, for karma is a faithful
Visitor and evil— a tree that never bears good fruit.

Final Words...

Every poem entitles itself, for in the skin of every
snake lies its name and its venom too. Fear not,
my son, trouble not your soul with thoughts of
what tomorrow will bring. Like the fireflies of the night,
Every man embodies his (own) lamp. Strive, think
Work and plant not your future in the farm of fate.
Work and pray, for today is a dream and tomorrow, a
firefly. Trouble not your soul with lengthy thoughts
For life is war, war is fire and fire is lamp and lamp
Is light. And light, the pathfinder in the time of night.

"If you can keep your head when all about you
Are losing theirs and blaming it on you,
If you can trust yourself when all men doubt you,
But make allowance for their doubting too;
If you can wait and not be tired of waiting
Or being lied upon, don't deal in lies,
Or being hated, don't give way to hating

The Letter

And yet don't look too good, nor talk too wise.
If you can dream— and not make dreams your master,
If you can think— and not make thought your aim
If you can meet Triumph and Disaster
And treat these two imposters just the same;
If you can bear to hear the truth you've spoken
Twisted by knaves to make a trap for fools
Or watch the things you gave your life to, broken
And stoop and build them up with worn-out tools:
If you can make one heap of all your winnings
And risk it on one turn of pitch-and-toss
And lose, and start again at your beginning
And never breathe a word about your loss;
If you can force your heart and nerve and sinew
To serve your turn long after they are gone.
And so hold on when there is nothing in you
Except the will which says to them: "Hold on!"
If you can talk with crowds and keep your virtue
Or walk with kings— nor lose the common touch.
If neither foes nor loving friends can hurt you,
If all men count with you, but none too much;
If you can fill the unforgiving minute
With sixty seconds worth of distance run,

Yours is the Earth and everything that's in it,

And— which is more— you'll be a Man, my son! "

-------**Rudyard Kipling**

My son, I hereby end this long letter, with these: Do not forget

that we (humans) are but leaves on this tree called earth, when

one's Chi calls, through the voice of the wind, without hesitation

he goes. When my Chi calls, I, too, must answer, for no one can

say no to the call of time, for we are but leaves on this tree called

earth. Do not fear that which makes all men lie still, for death is

not the swollen silence that coats us with cruel cold. Death is not

the stillness of sense that gives breath long walk to unfold. Death is not the sudden end of breath, Death is the ignorance of life's

purpose that makes great men live a dead life.

My son, I hope this letter helps you to find peace in this world

of woes. I hope it directs your feet to achieve your dreams, I hope it gives you succor and comfort when I lie still and silent

in the beautiful box of bliss: the last home of things that breathe.

Son, when a load leaves the head, the shoulder bears the load.

My son, death makes a daughter mother and a son the father of his father's house. As I journey down the stream, father my house

Let not an antelope march into the lion's lair demanding a debt.

Your beloved father

Samuel Alozie Onyeche

+2348131181492

Glossary

Ajuala: A gentle and patient kind of African viper but very deadly when its life is threatened.

Amadioha: The god of Thunder known to be among the most powerful gods in Western Africa.

Odu and Ebi: Grasscutter and Porcupine (animals)

Imgullible*: (coinage) Difficult to be tricked or deceived.

Thánatos: the Greek word for death

Eyeswater. Poetically used to depict tears.

Farmfly: Housefly of the farm.

Mturufe: a West African trap that is hidden in the ground, it is used to capture smart animals.

Chi: An Igbo/ Etchie word that refers to One's personal god (a divine entity that guides and protects an individual)

About the Author

Samuel Onyeche

The Poet, Philosopher, and a Creative Writer.

SAMUEL ONYECHE is an extraordinary poet, an aphorist, and a creative African writer from the Niger Delta region of Nigeria. He has received several honours and awards, such as 2nd position Prof. Kontein Trinya's Poetry Prize 2016, "Most Creative" National Youth Service Corps Theatre Troupe Award (2020) Sokoto State, Poet of the Day Award (2022), award from Global Poetic Pen International, Certificate of Excellence from the Temple of Impeccable Writers. Certificate of Excellence 2018 from the department of English and Literary Studies, Ignatius Ajuru University of Education, Port Harcourt, Nigeria, and many others.

Onyeche's works have also been featured in many international anthologies namely: Tamikio L. Dooley's Pens of Artists 2022, United States of America, Poets for Peace Poetry Anthology, Tunisia 2022, Cooch Behar Indian Anthology 2022. He has the following books to his name: Ijikrika; Canticles From Africa, On the Wings of a Butterfly, A Casserole of Kisses (co-authored), Parasites in Paradise, Echoes of Kettledrums(co-authored), One Hundred Aphorisms of Life, The Muse of Love (co-authored) Song of My Country and many other books which are all on Amazon. He holds a Bachelor of Education Degree (B.ED) in English and Literary Studies and a Masters of Arts Degree (M.A) in literature from the Ignatius Ajuru University of Education, Port Harcourt, Nigeria.

You can get in touch with him on +2348131181492. Or samuel4godonyeche@gmail.com

Books by the Author

1. Paradise in Paradise. (Niger Delta Poetry) 2018

2. On the Wings of a Butterfly. (Love and Romance) 2020

3. Ijikrika; Canticles from Africa. 2022

4. Song of my Country. 2023

5. A Casserole of Kisses. (Co-authored) 2023

6. Echoes of Kettledrum (Co-authored) 2023

7. One Hundred Aphorisms of Life. 2023

8. The Muse of Love (Co-authored)

9. The Hidden Truth; Dangers, Beauty, and Secrets of AI. 2023

10. One Hundred Aphorisms of Life; Volume 2. 2023

www.ingramcontent.com/pod-product-compliance
Lightning Source LLC
LaVergne TN
LVHW041553070526
838199LV00046B/1940